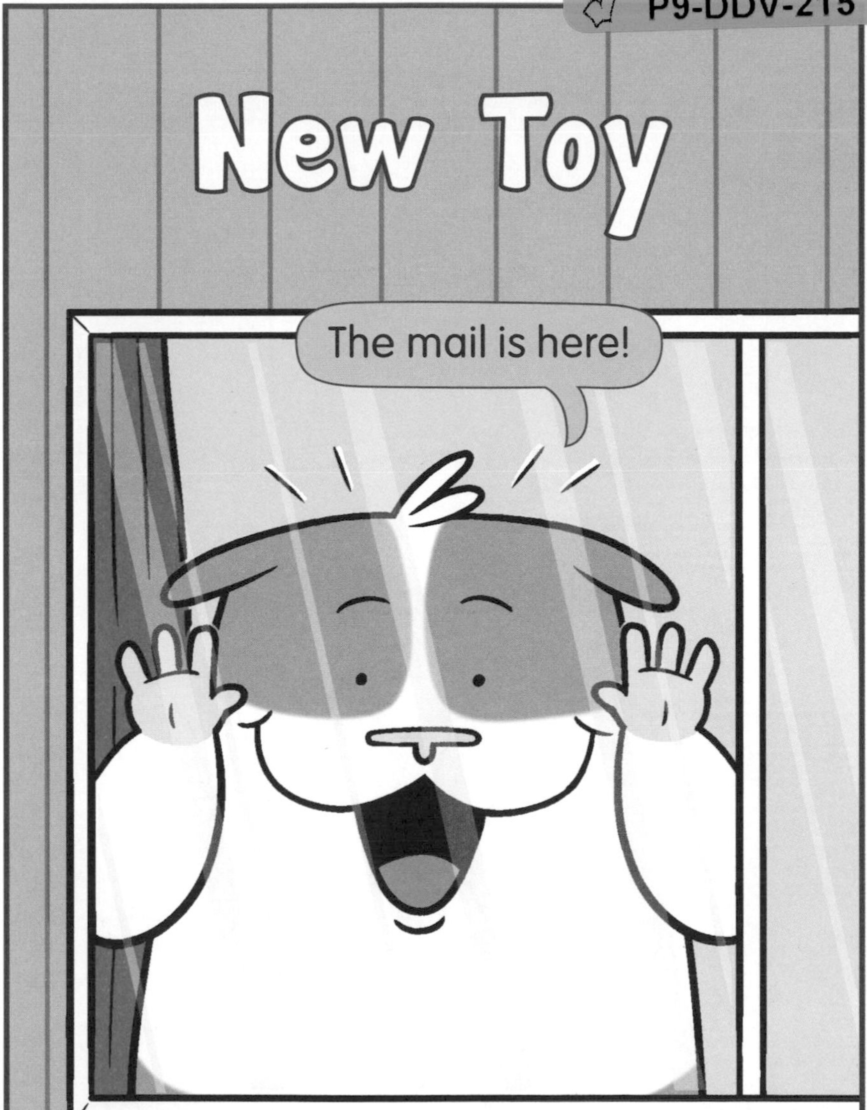
New Toy
The mail is here!

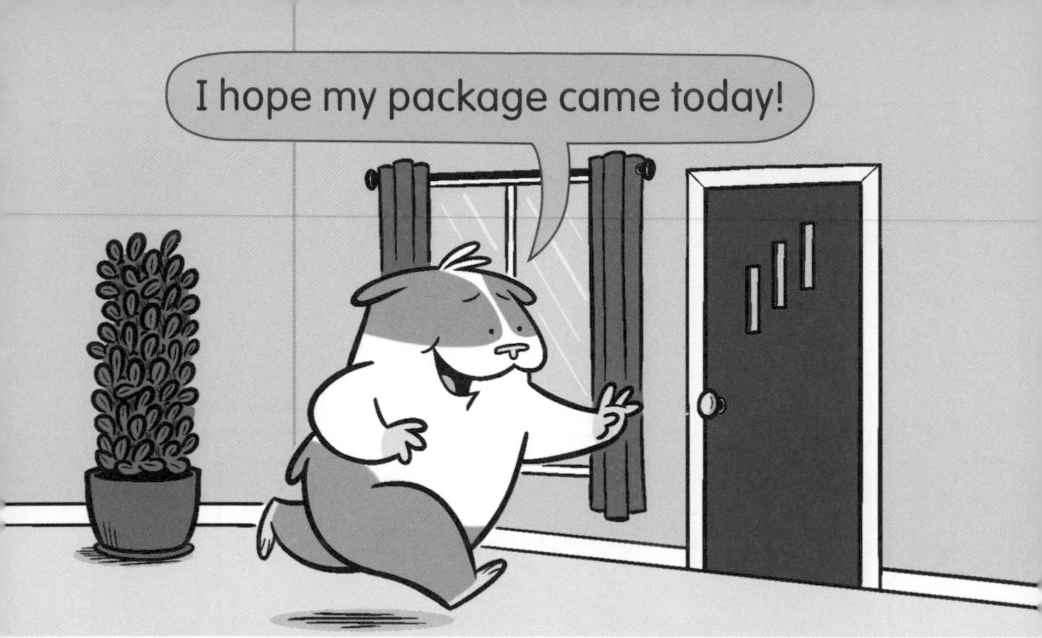
I hope my package came today!

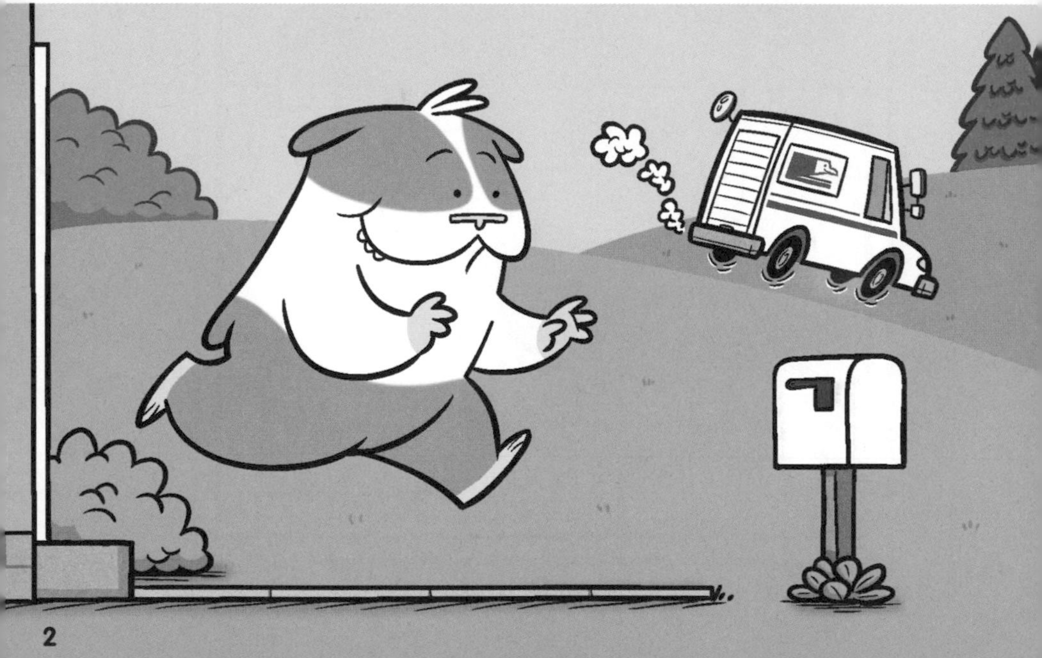

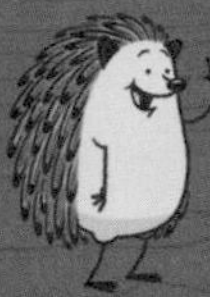

HELLO, HEDGEHOG!™

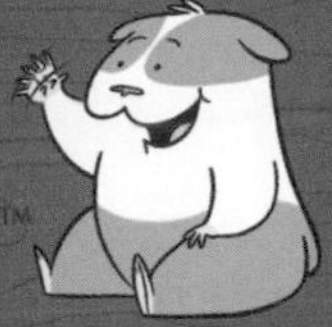

Can I Have a Turn?

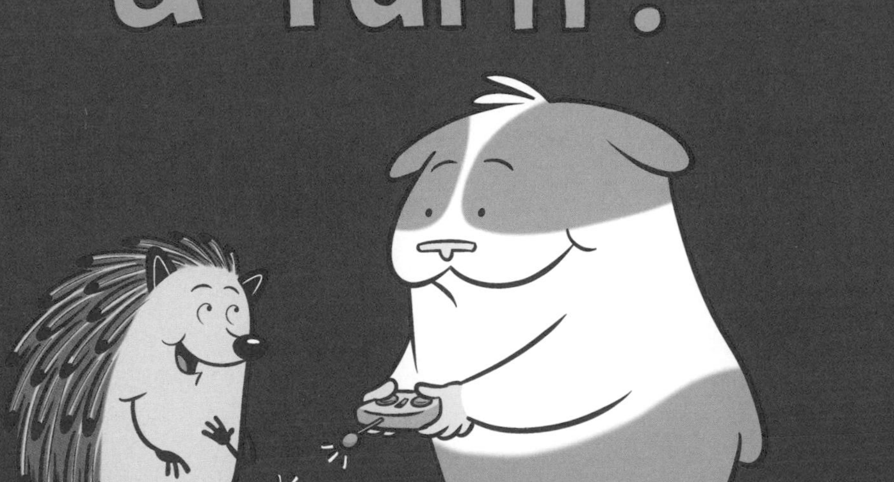

ACORN™
SCHOLASTIC INC.

Norm Feuti

For Charlotte and Ben —NF

Library of Congress Cataloging-in-Publication Data

Names: Feuti, Norman, author, illustrator.
Title: Can I have a turn? / Norm Feuti.
Description: First edition. | New York : Acorn/Scholastic Inc., 2022. |
Series: Hello, Hedgehog! ; 5 | Summary: After Harry receives a new toy car in the mail, Harry and Hedgehog have fun taking turns racing the car around the racetrack Harry built.
Identifiers: LCCN 2021001276 (print) | ISBN 9781338677140 (paperback) |
ISBN 9781338677157 (library binding) |
Subjects: CYAC: Hedgehogs—Fiction. | Sharing—Fiction. | Toys—Fiction. |
Friendship—Fiction.
Classification: LCC PZ7.1.F52 Can 2022 (print) |
DDC [E]—dc23

LC record available at https://lccn.loc.gov/2021001276

10 9 8 7 6 5 4 3 2 1   22 23 24 25 26

Printed in China   62
First edition, February 2022
Edited by Katie Carella
Book design by Maria Mercado

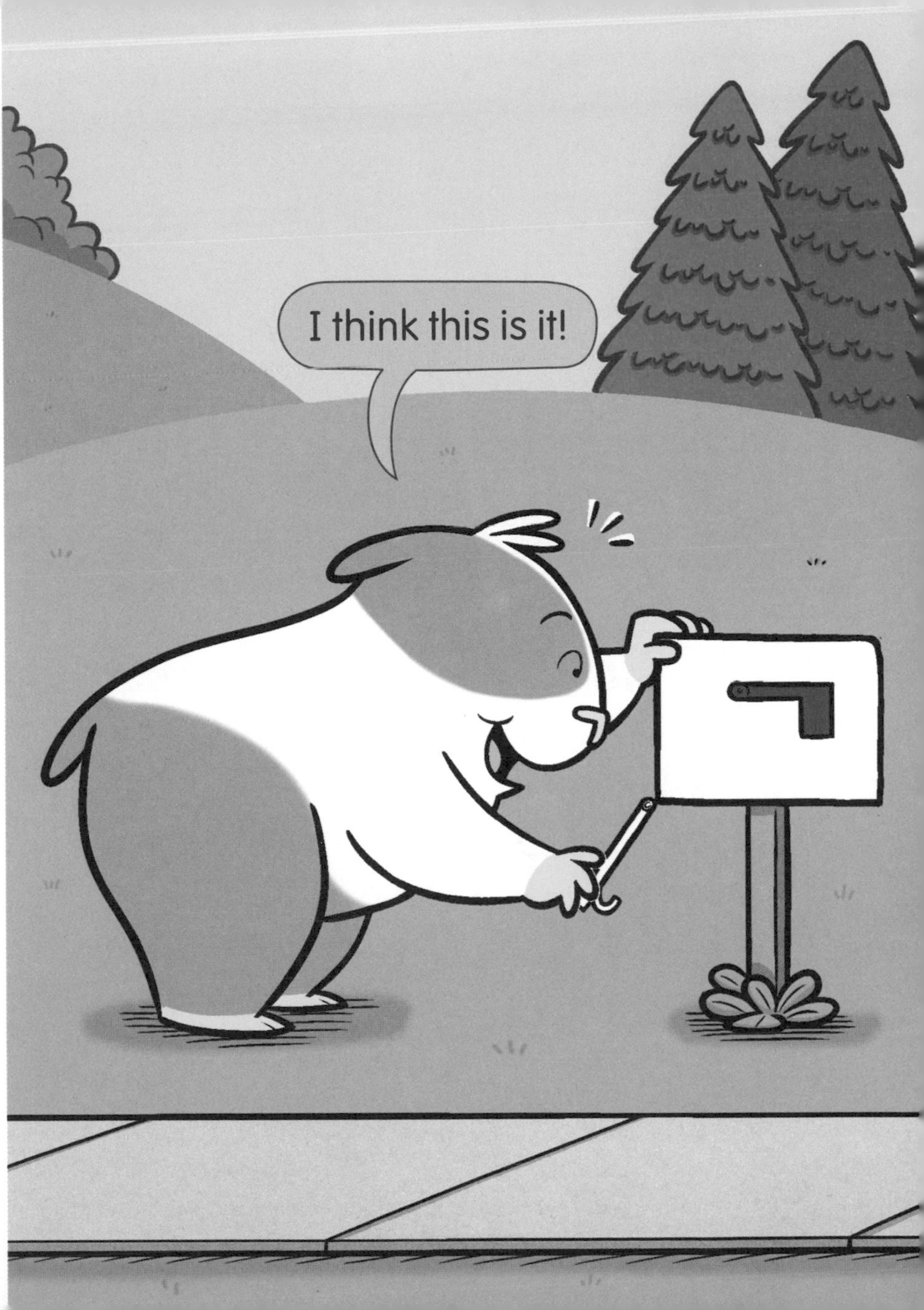
I think this is it!

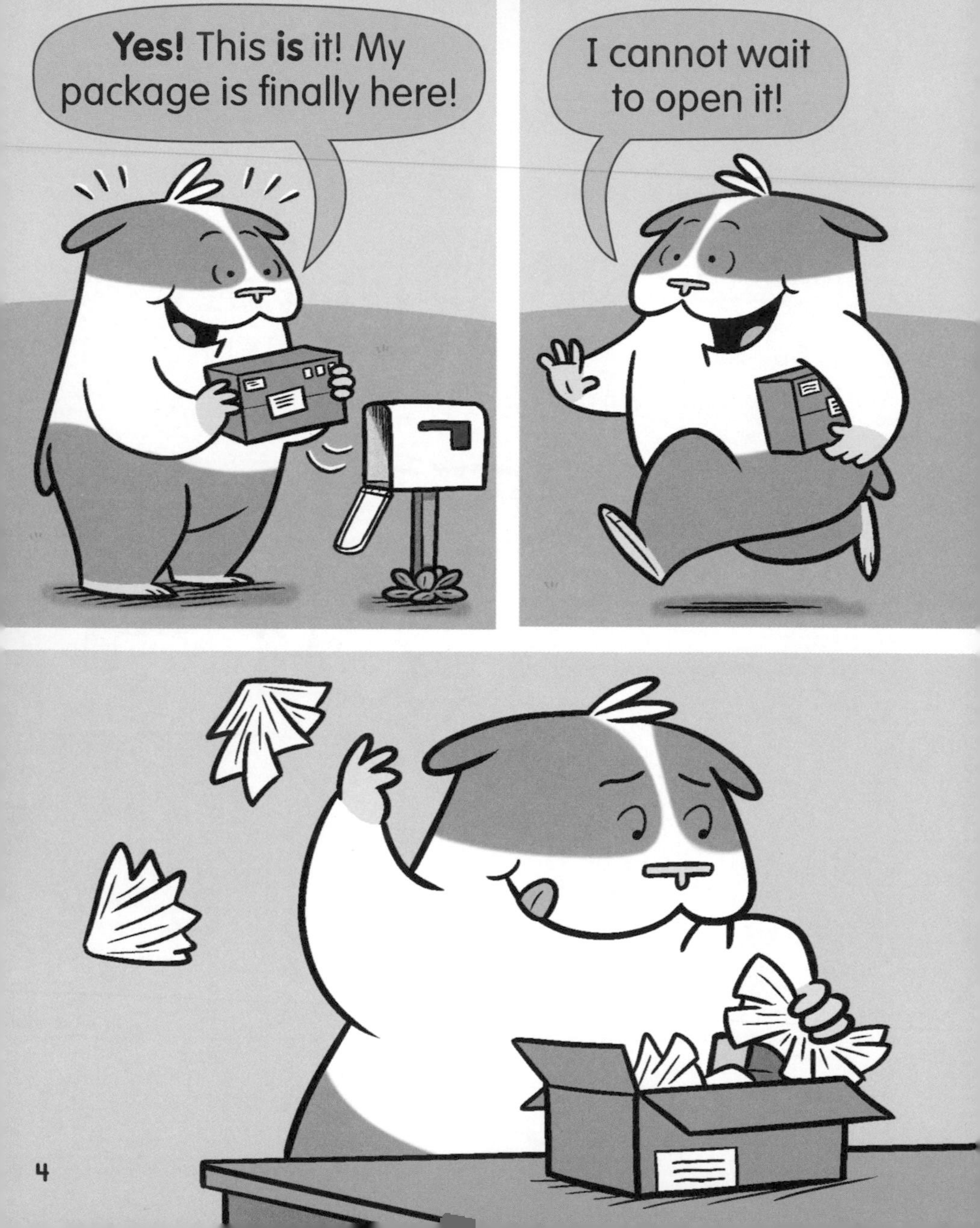
Yes! This **is** it! My package is finally here!
I cannot wait to open it!

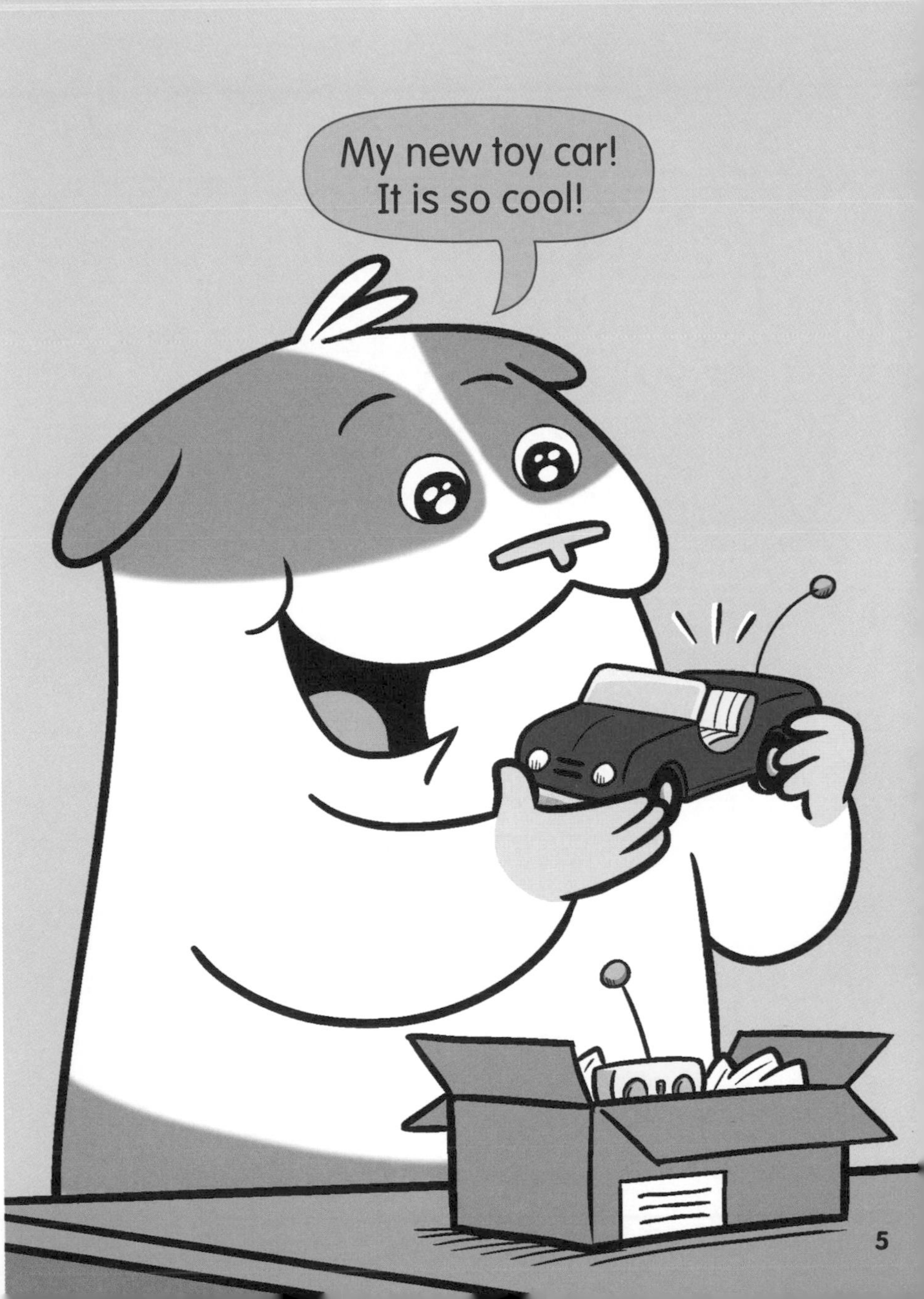
My new toy car!
It is so cool!

7

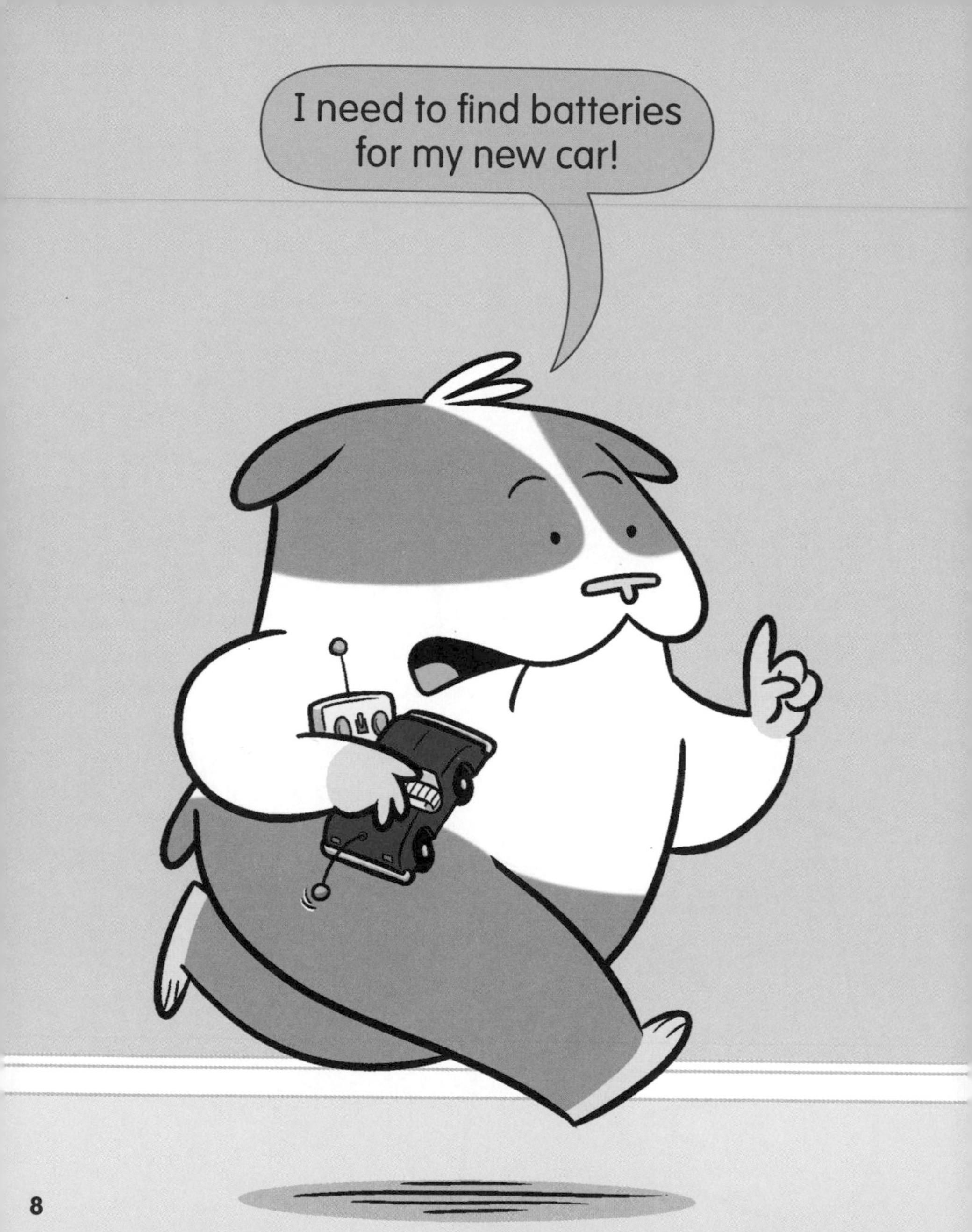
I need to find batteries for my new car!

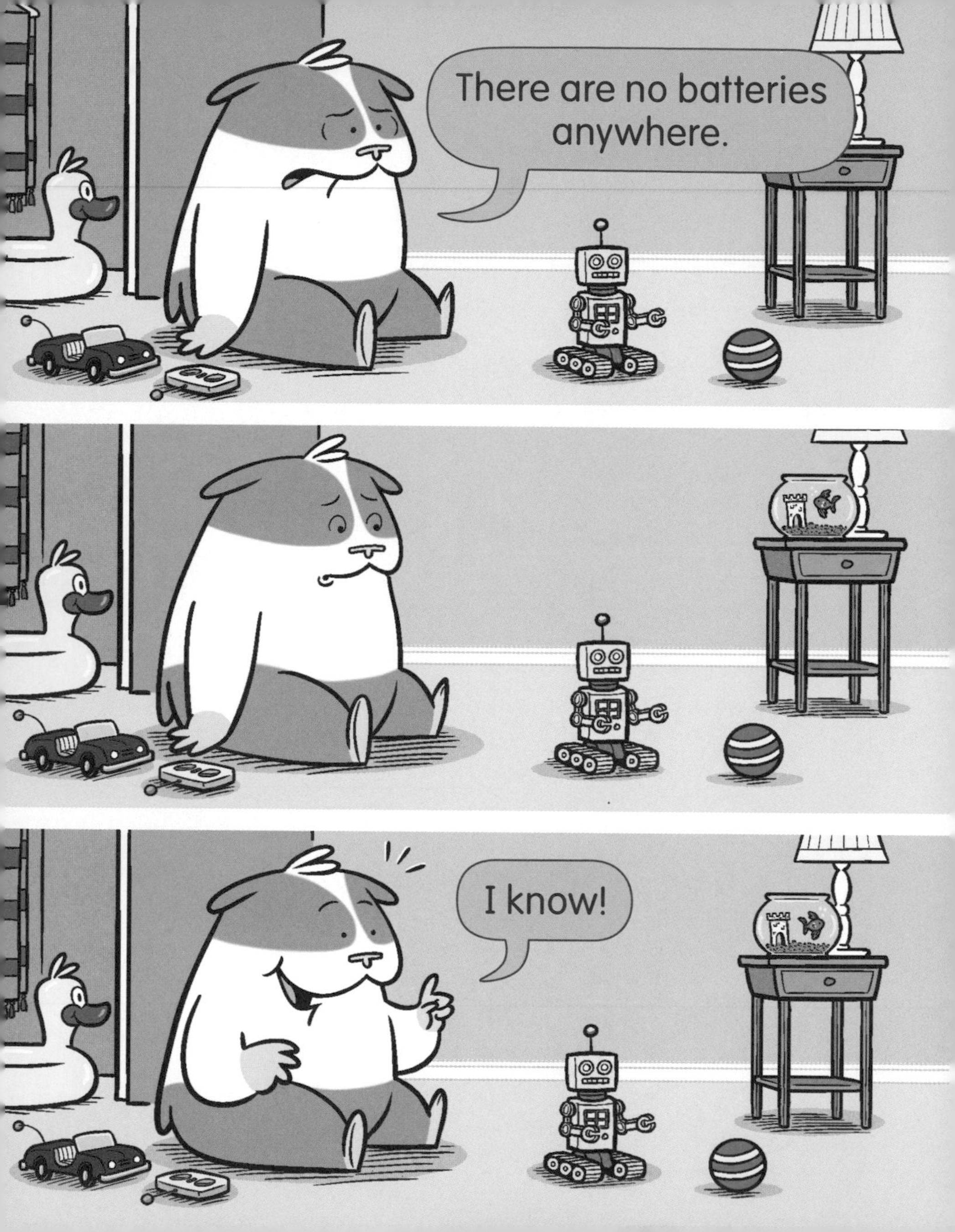
There are no batteries anywhere.
I know!

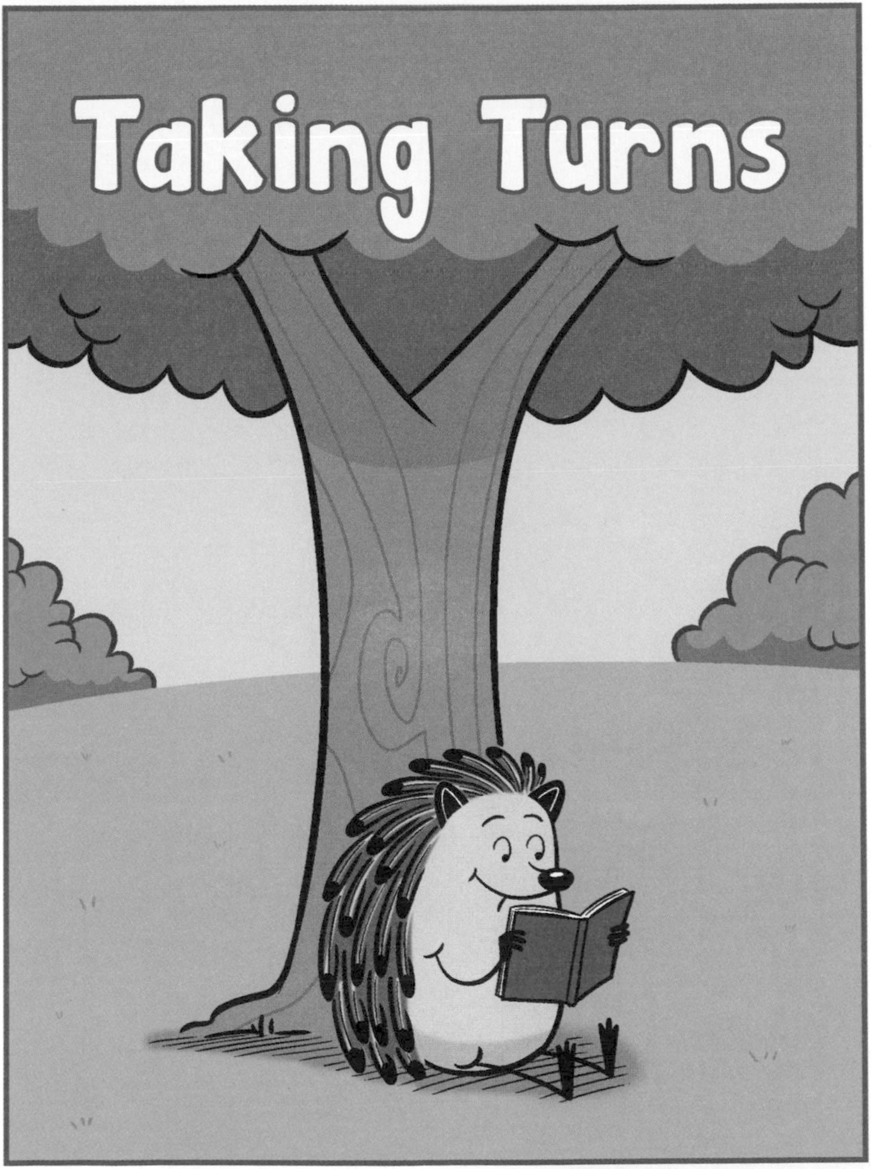
Taking Turns

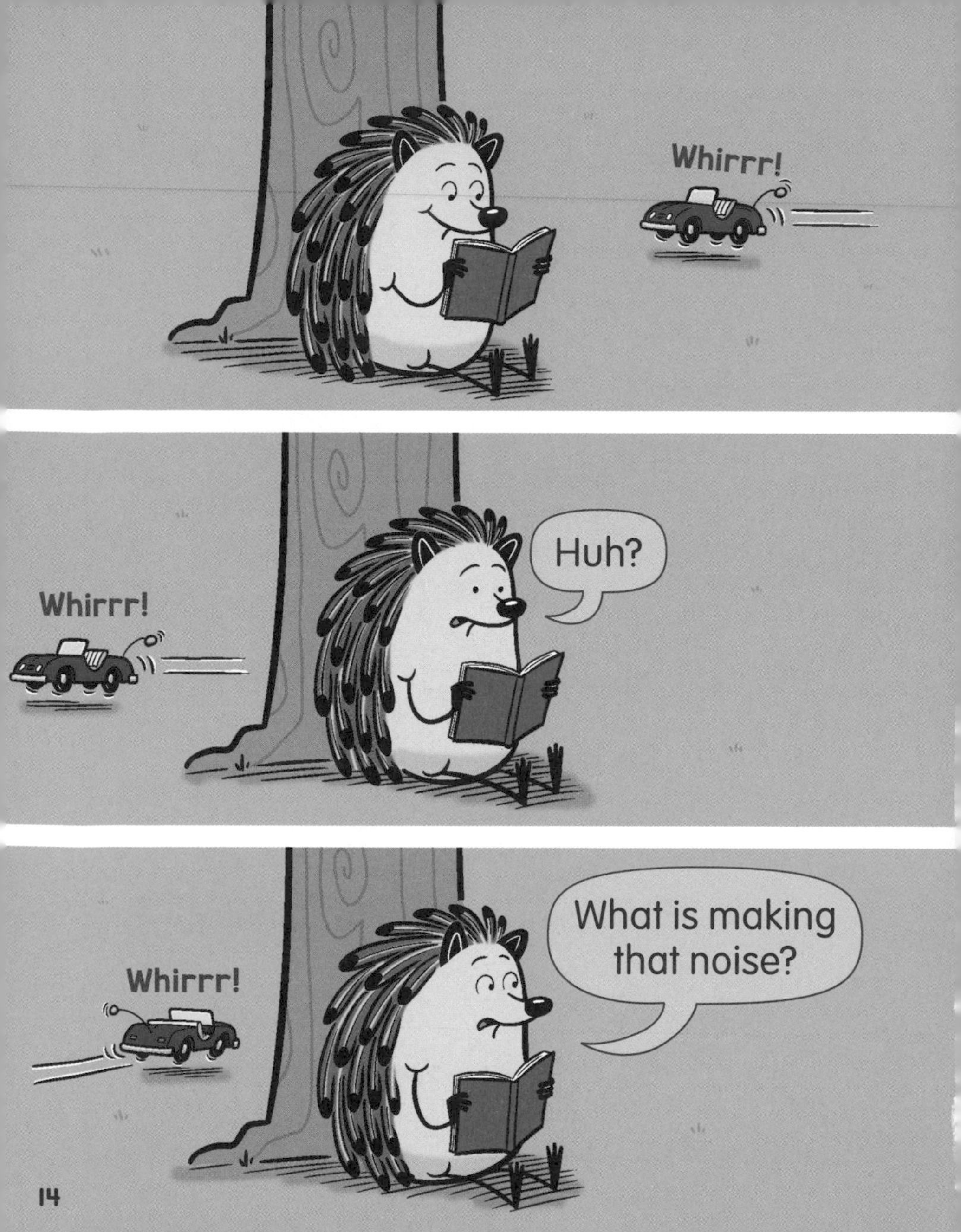
Whirrr!
Whirrr!
Huh?
Whirrr!
What is making that noise?

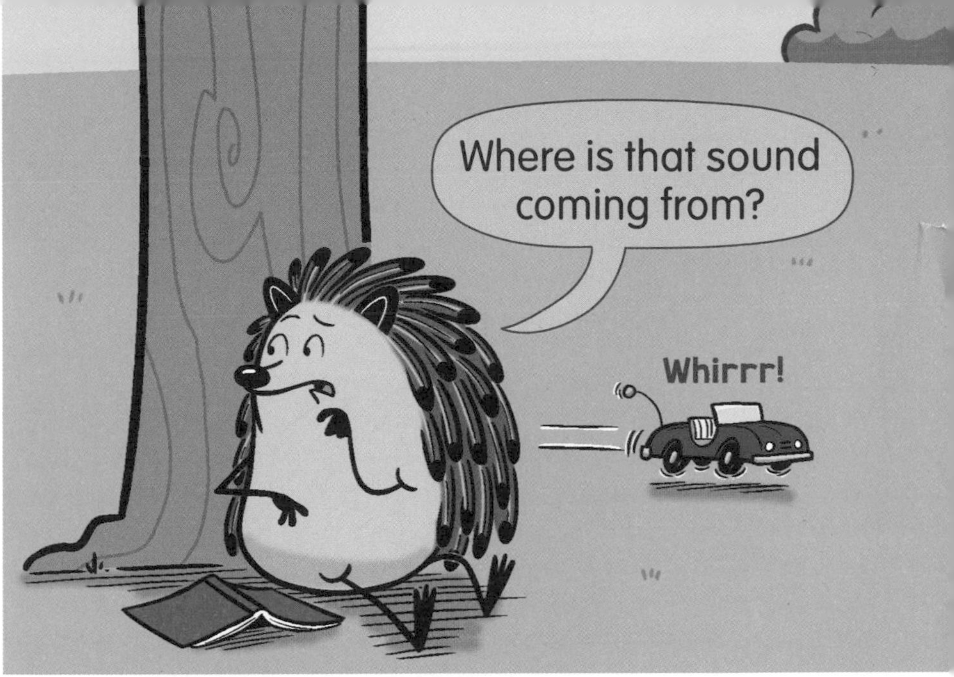
Where is that sound coming from?
Whirrr!

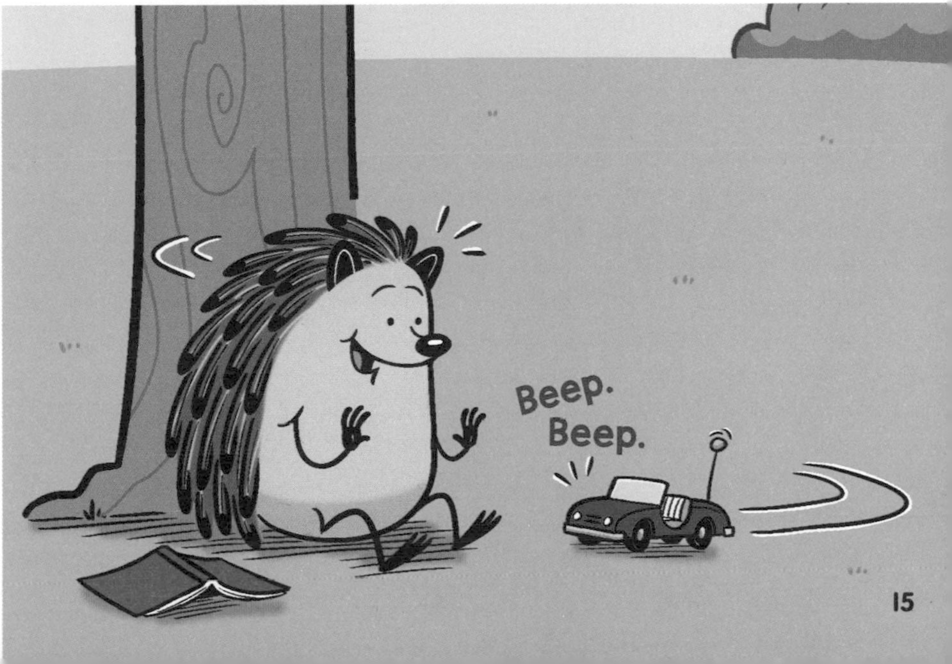
Beep.
Beep.

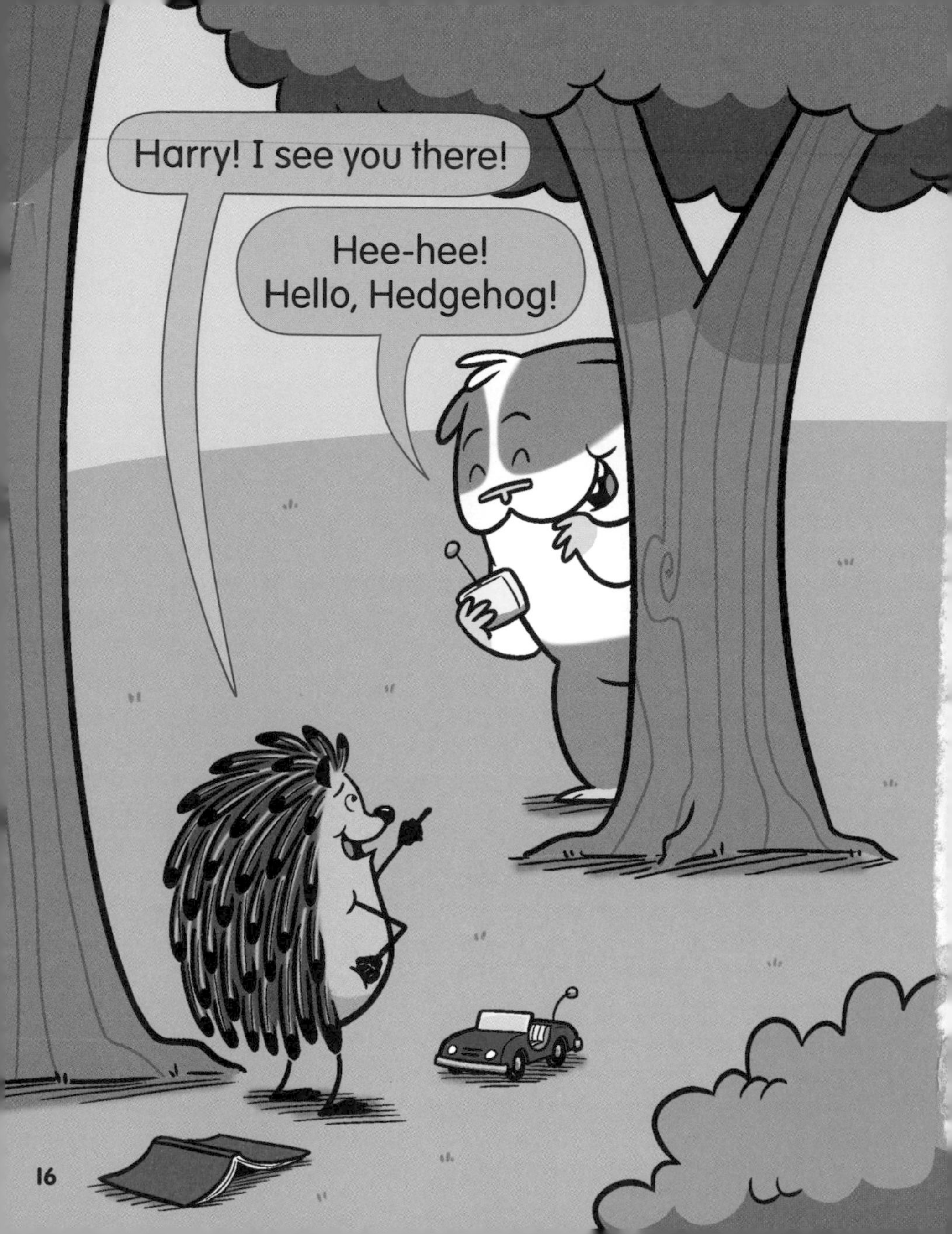
Harry! I see you there!
Hee-hee!
Hello, Hedgehog!

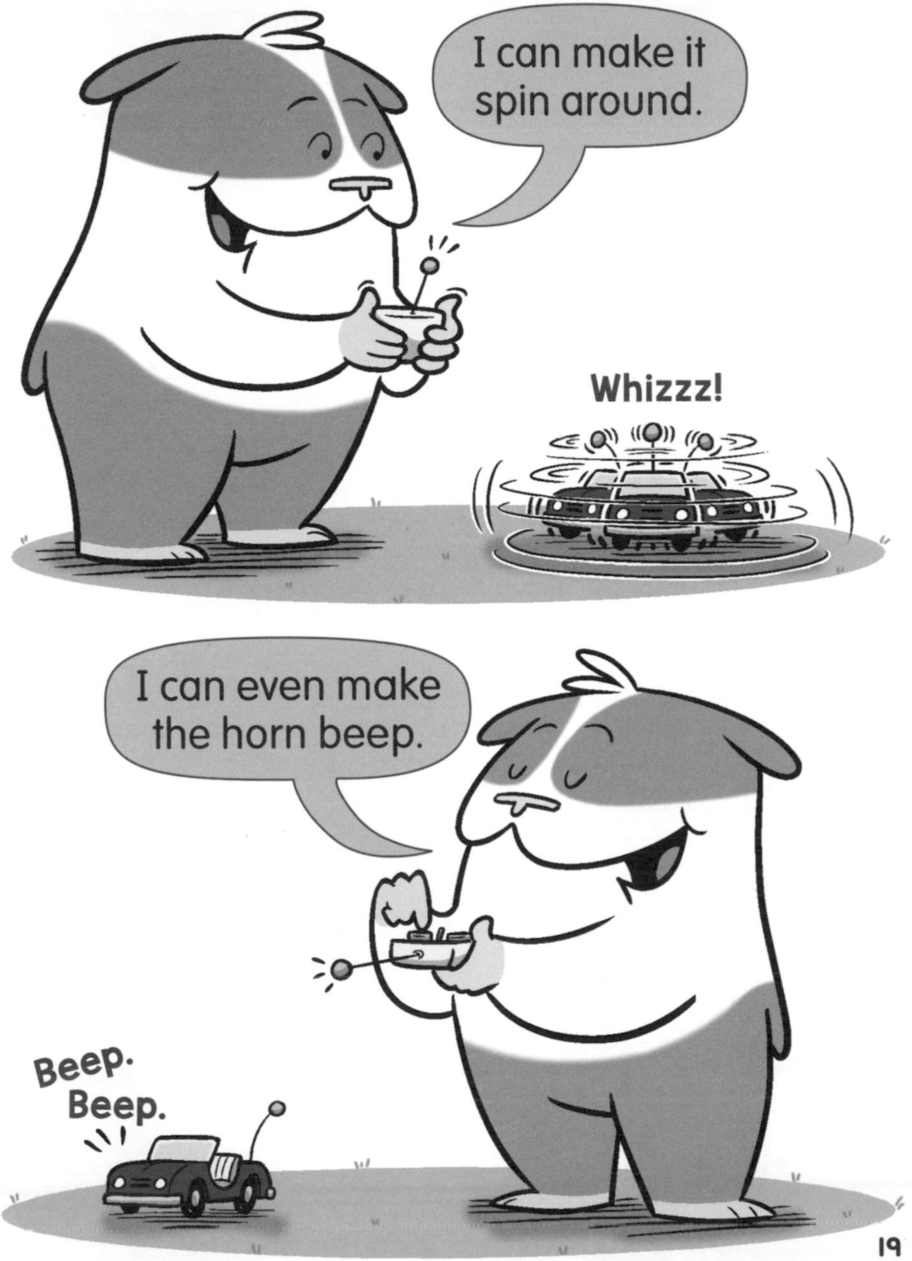
I can make it spin around.
Whizzz!
I can even make the horn beep.
Beep. Beep.

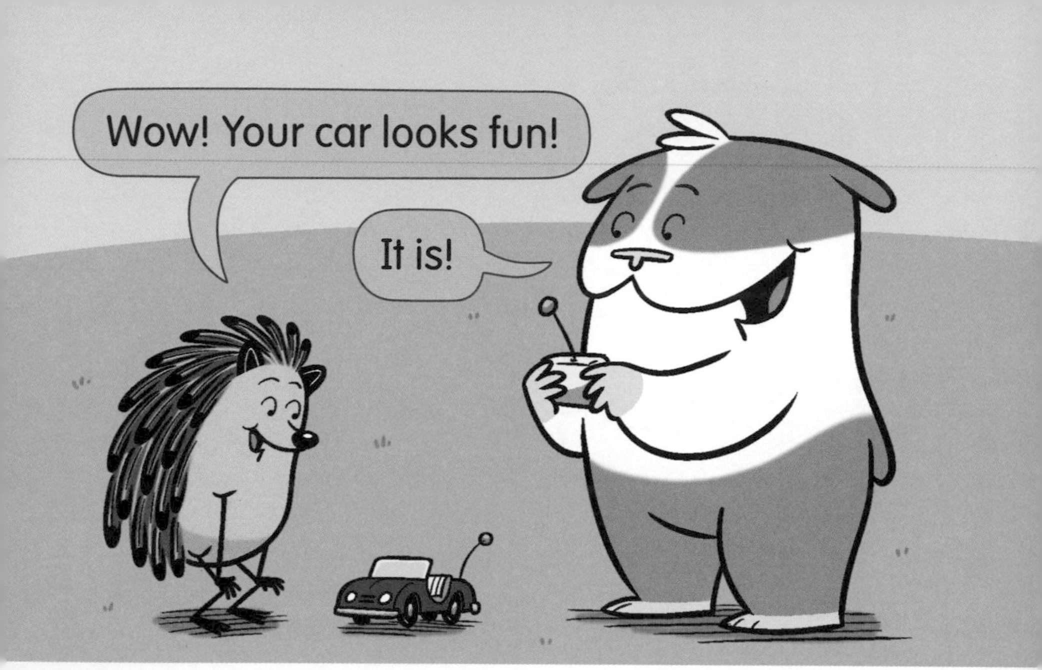
Wow! Your car looks fun!
It is!

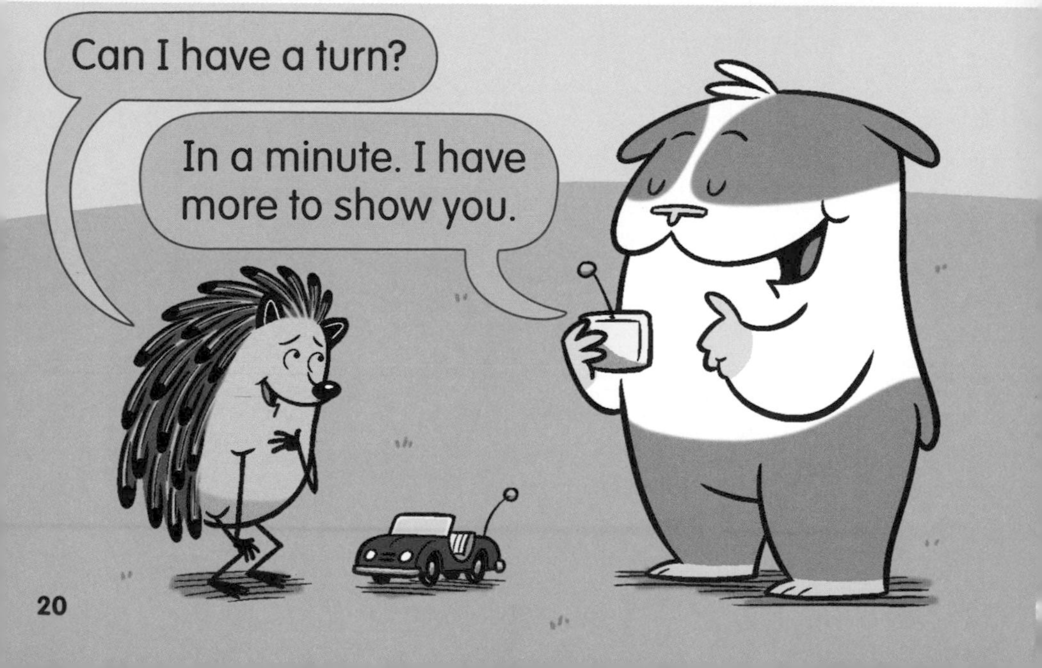
Can I have a turn?
In a minute. I have more to show you.

21

22

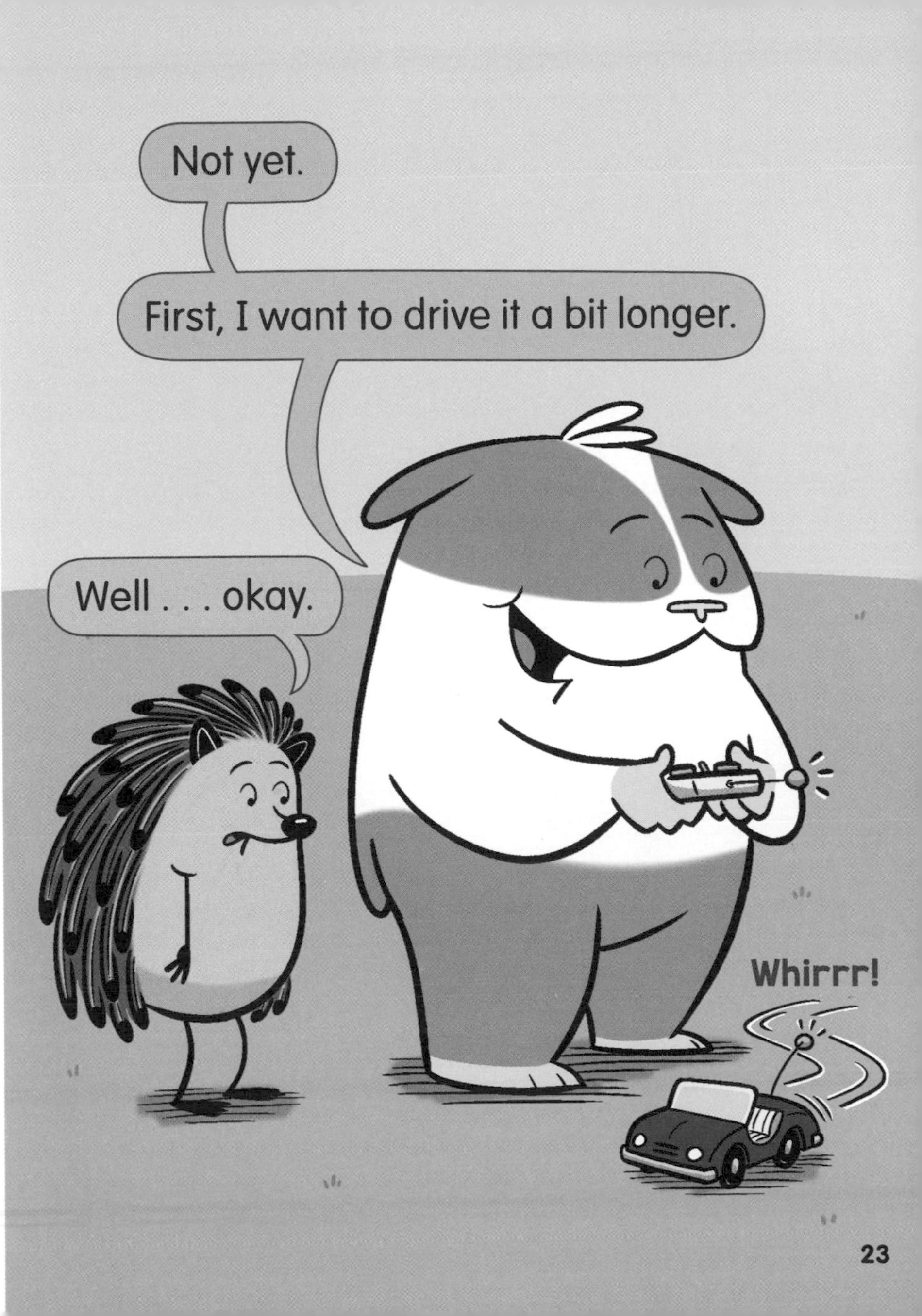
Not yet.
First, I want to drive it a bit longer.
Well . . . okay.
Whirrr!

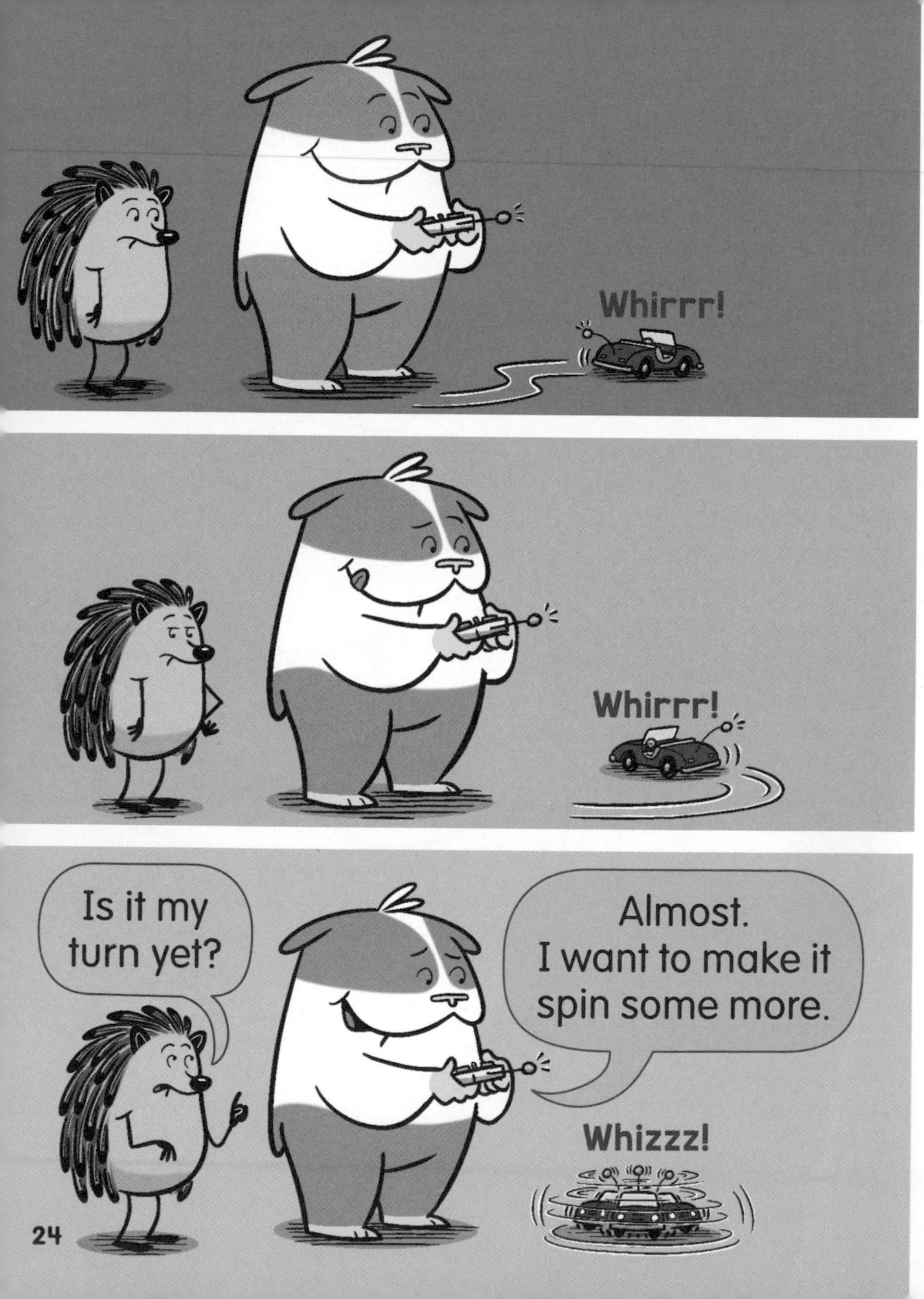
Whirrr!
Whirrr!
Is it my turn yet?
Almost. I want to make it spin some more.
Whizzz!

25

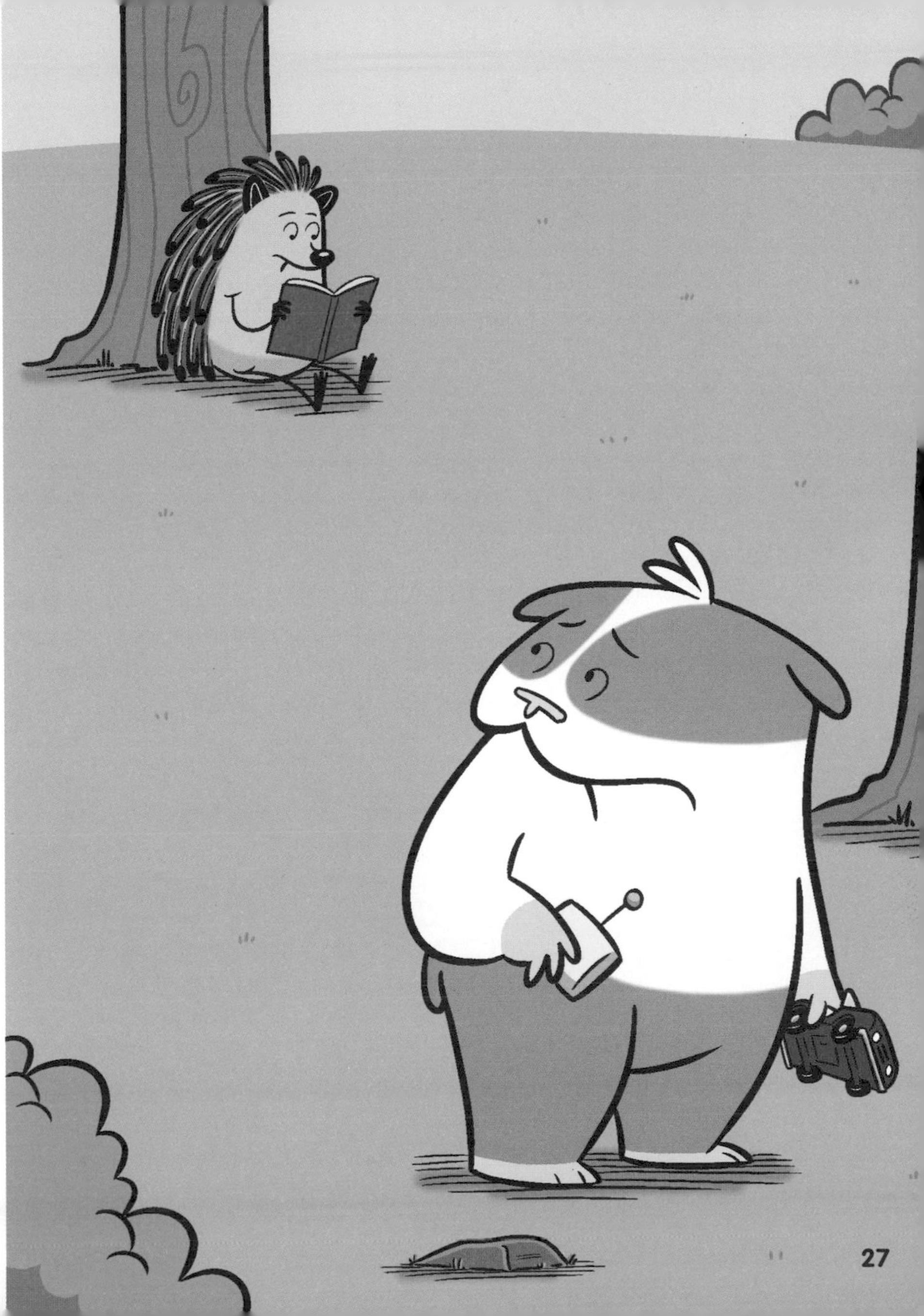

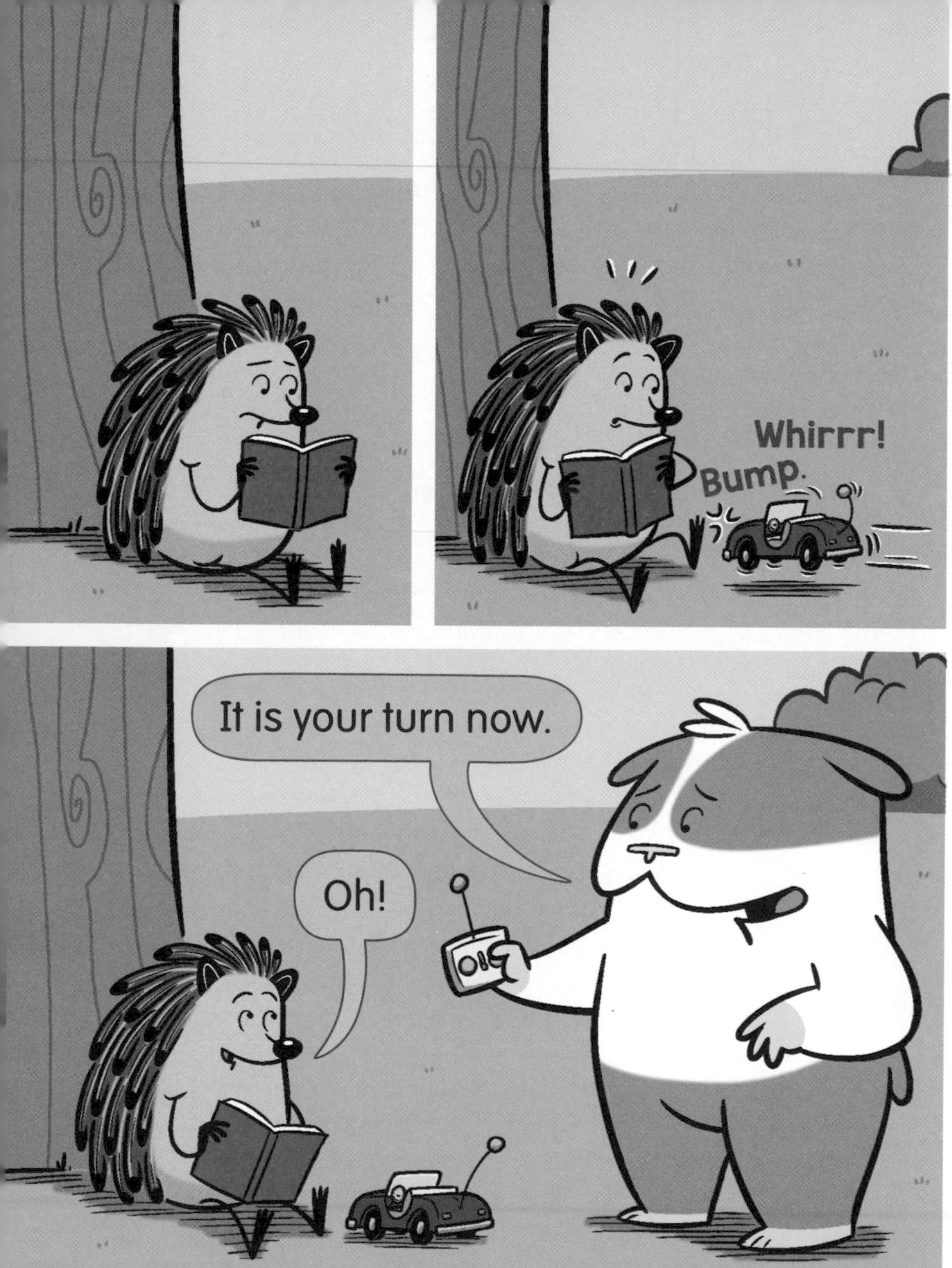
Whirrr!
Bump.
It is your turn now.
Oh!

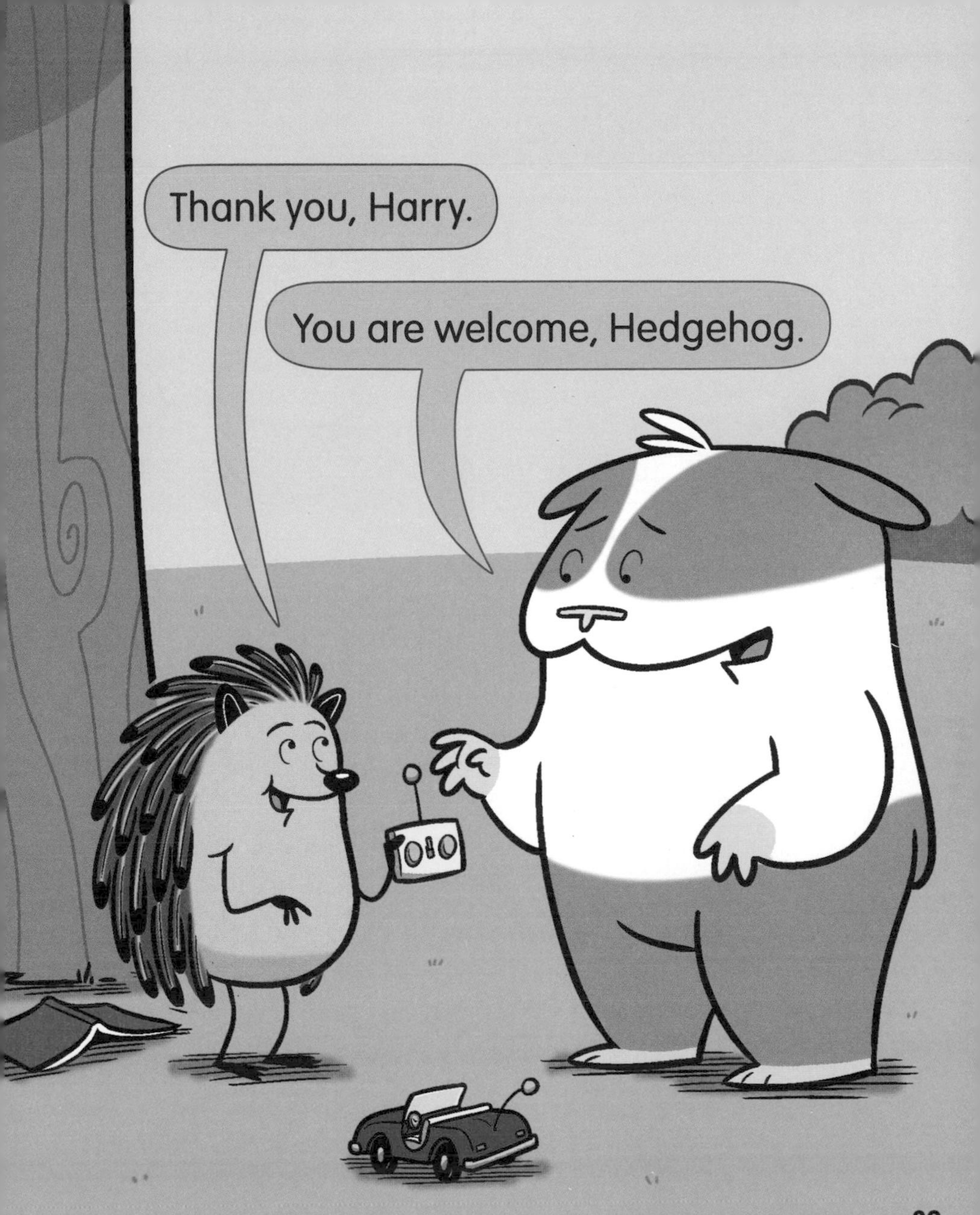
Thank you, Harry.
You are welcome, Hedgehog.

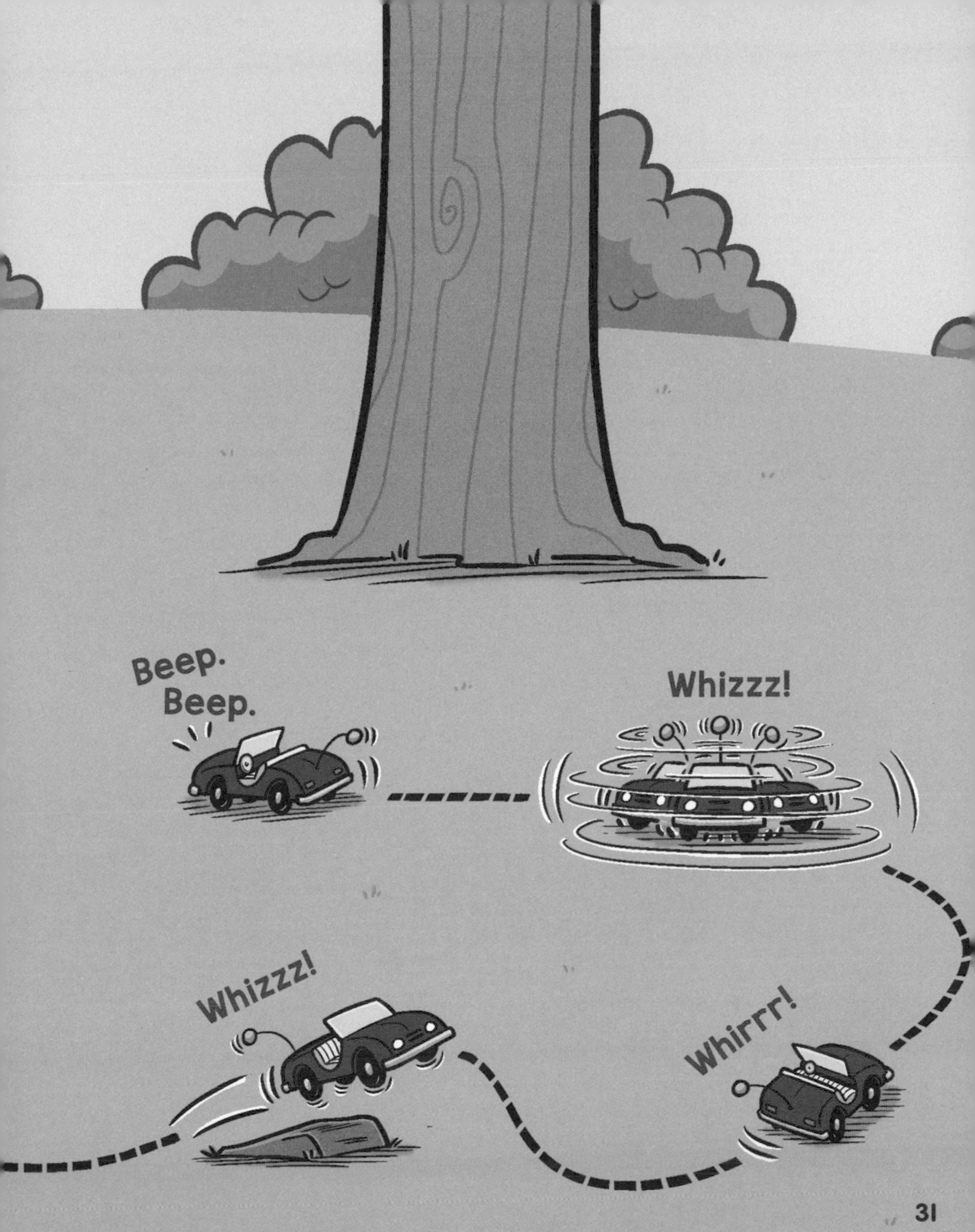

Beep.
Beep.
Whizzz!
Whizzz!
Whirrr!

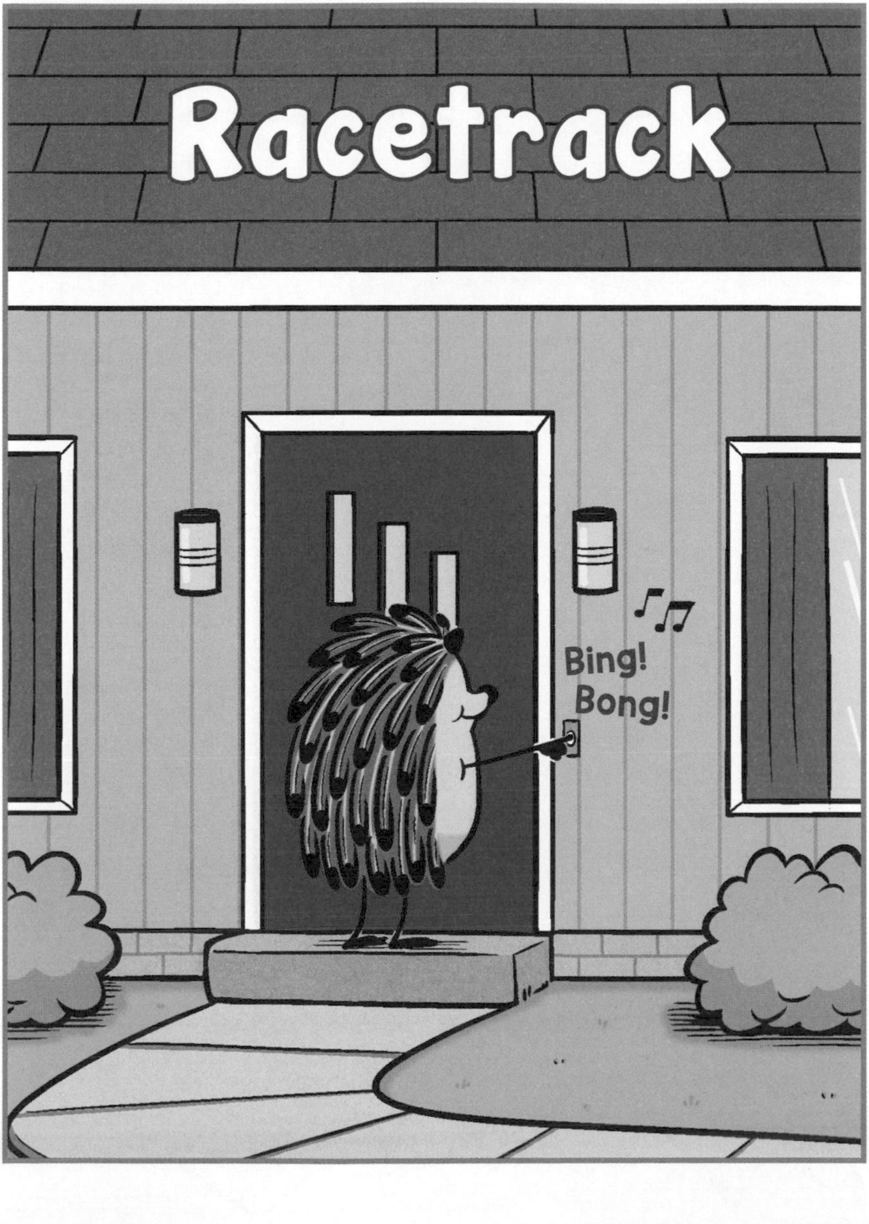
Racetrack
Bing!
Bong!

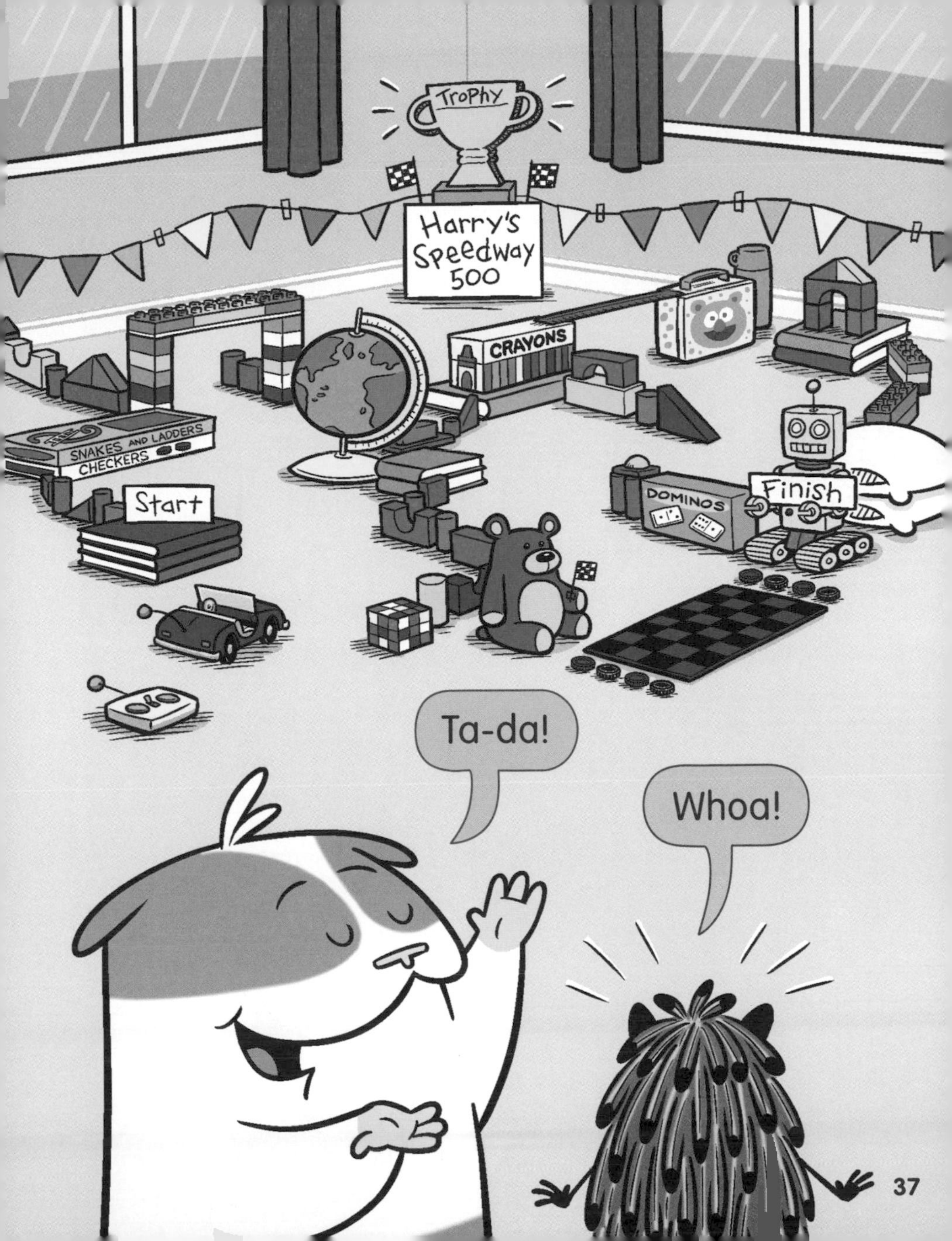
Trophy
Harry's Speedway 500
CRAYONS
SNAKES AND LADDERS
CHECKERS
Start
DOMINOS
Finish
Ta-da!
Whoa!

I made a racetrack!
We can take turns driving
my toy car around it.
This is so cool!
We will time each other —
And whoever goes around
fastest will be the winner!

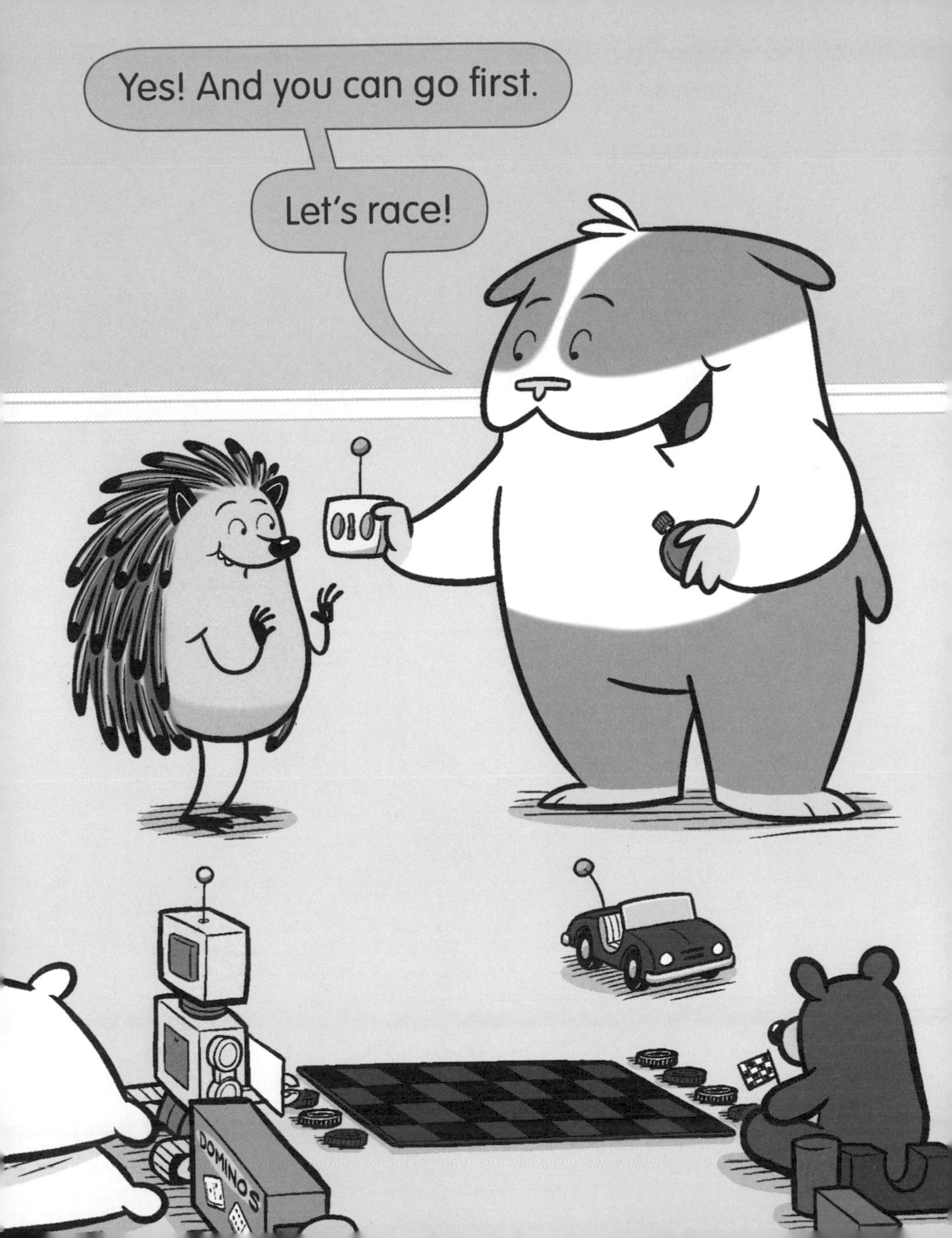
Yes! And you can go first.
Let's race!
DOMINOS

41

44

About the Author

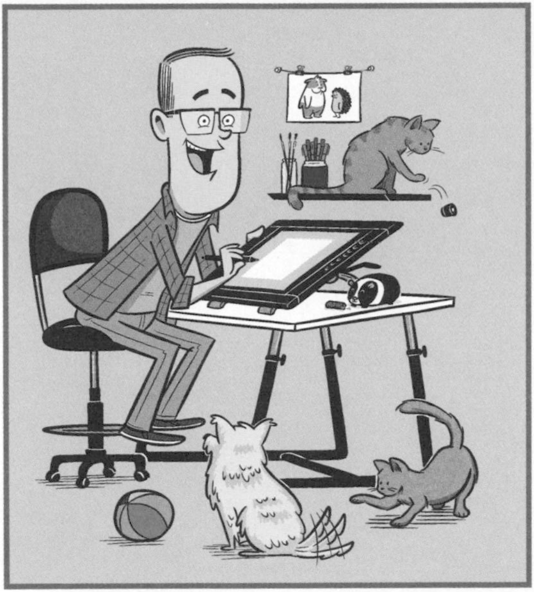

Norm Feuti lives in Massachusetts with his family, a dog, two cats, and a guinea pig. He is the creator of the newspaper comic strips **Retail** and **Gil**. He is also the author and illustrator of the graphic novel **The King of Kazoo**. **Hello, Hedgehog!** is Norm's first early reader series.

YOU CAN DRAW A CAR!

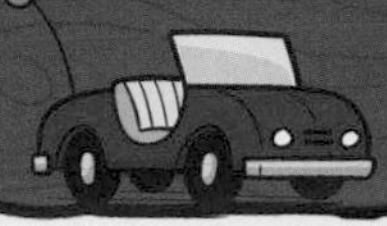

1. Draw a rectangle with round edges on top.

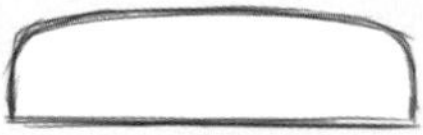

2. Draw three half circles inside the rectangle. Then draw a curved line to make the car's hood.

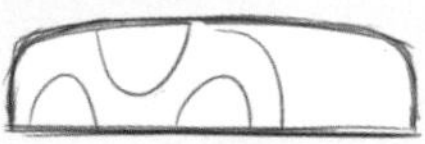

3. Add wheels! Draw four half circles below the rectangle. Then add a windshield on top of the rectangle.

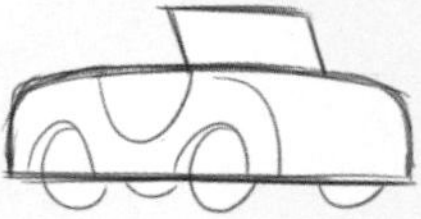

4. Draw two headlights. Then add bumpers — one on the front and one on the back.

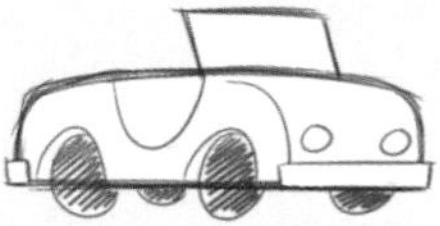

5. Add the seat. Draw details on the hood. Then add an antenna to the back of the car.

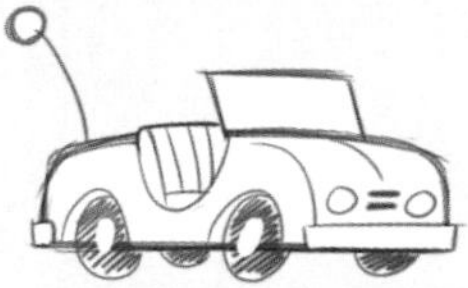

6. Color in your drawing!

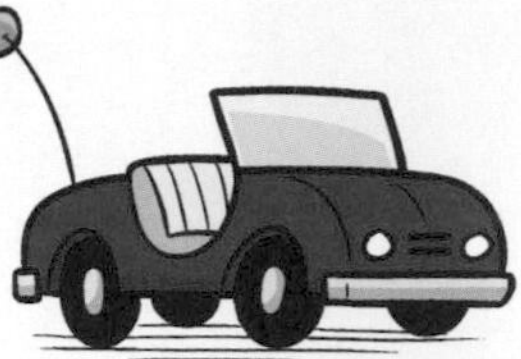

WHAT'S YOUR STORY?

Harry races a toy car with Hedgehog.
Imagine Harry asks **you** to build a racetrack.
Where would you build it?
What things would you use?
Write and draw your story!

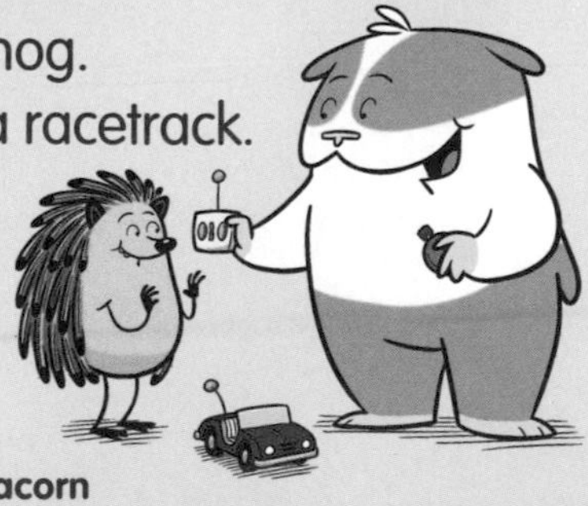

scholastic.com/acorn